All of a sudden, the girls heard a loud gasp coming from the kitchen.

"What was that?" Mary asked.

Nancy looked at Bess and George. "It was Hannah! Let's go see what's happening! Come on!"

Hannah Gruen was the Drews' house-keeper. She had been with the family ever since Nancy's mother had died five years before. Nancy was positive that Hannah was the best cook in River Heights. She was also sure that Hannah gave the best hugs.

When the girls got to the kitchen, Hannah was just getting off the phone.

"Are you all right?" Nancy asked.

Hannah turned and looked at them. "I just got off the phone with Mr. Madison," she said sadly. "It looks like Thanksgiving won't be the same this year!"

Join the CLUE CREW
& solve these other cases!

REW

#16 AND THE CLUE CREW®

Thanksgiving Thief

BY CAROLYN KEENE

ILLUSTRATED BY MACKY PAMINTUAN

Aladdin Paperbacks
New York London Toronto Sydney

This book is a work of fiction. Any references to historical events, real people, or real locales are used fictitiously. Other names, characters, places, and incidents are the product of the author's imagination, and any resemblance to actual events or locales or persons, living or dead, is entirely coincidental.

ALADDIN PAPERBACKS

An imprint of Simon & Schuster Children's Publishing Division

1230 Avenue of the Americas, New York, NY 10020

Text copyright © 2008 by Simon & Schuster, Inc.

Illustrations copyright © 2008 Macky Pamintuan

All rights reserved, including the right of reproduction in whole or in part in any form.

NANCY DREW, NANCY DREW AND THE CLUE CREW, ALADDIN PAPERBACKS, and related logo are registered trademarks of Simon & Schuster, Inc.

Designed by Lisa Vega

The text of this book was set in ITC Stone Informal.

Manufactured in the United States of America

First Aladdin Paperbacks edition September 2008

20 19 18 17 16 15 14

Library of Congress Control Number 2007943606

ISBN-13: 978-1-4169-6777-4

ISBN-13: 978-1-4424-5920-5 (eBook)

0316 OFF

CONTENTS

Thanksgiving Thief

ChAPTER ONE

Cool Costumes

"Those poor turkeys!" eight-year-old Nancy Drew said. She was watching a story on the small television set in her room. "Someone needs to help them."

"What are you talking about?" asked Bess Marvin.

Nancy explained that some wild turkeys had been spotted in the parking lot of River Heights Elementary School late yesterday afternoon. When one of the school janitors tried to catch them, though, they ran away. No one was exactly sure where they had come from.

"I wonder why they were at our school," George Fayne said.

"The news showed them trying to drink some of the dirty water coming from a broken pipe," Nancy said. "I guess they were thirsty."

"Oh, poor things," Mary White Cloud said. "They need *clean* water to drink."

Nancy nodded. "It stinks that that broken pipe flooded some of the school offices, but I'm glad they canceled school today."

"Yeah! A three-day weekend!" exclaimed Bess. "We need the time to get ready for the pageant."

"Speaking of the pageant," George said, "we're all going to *be* turkeys if we don't pay more attention to what we're doing here."

Nancy giggled.

Bess twirled around in front of Nancy's mirror and looked at the beaded leather dress she was wearing. "I love being a Native American princess," she said. "This is so cool."

Mary White Cloud looked at Bess. "You look great!" she said.

Mary was a new girl in their class at school. She was Native American. The girls' teacher, Mrs.

Ramirez, had asked Mary to cast three more girls in the class to play Native American princesses in the pageant part of the River Heights Thanksgiving Celebration. Mary had chosen Nancy and Nancy's two best friends, Bess and George. Most of the time, everyone in River Heights knew the three of them as the Clue Crew. They solved mysteries in town that baffled everyone else. George and Bess were also cousins, although they weren't at all alike.

"The three of you are just right for the part. I hope this pageant is the best one ever at our school."

"We do too, Mary," Bess said. "Thanks for choosing us."

Nancy was always excited about the River Heights Thanksgiving Celebration. It was held at their school on the Wednesday before Thanksgiving. It gave the whole town a chance to celebrate the holiday together with a pageant, a feast, and a food fair.

"Now for the headbands," said Mary. She

opened a box on Nancy's bed and took out four beaded strips of leather. "These were worn by real Native American princesses in a tribal ceremony in Oklahoma last year," she told the other girls. "My uncle in Lawton sent them to me."

"Cool!" Nancy said. "Maybe they'll magically turn us into *real* princesses."

The four of them put on the headbands.

"Mine's a little tight," said Bess.

"That's because you have a big head," George joked.

"No, I don't," Bess retorted. "It's normal."

"Mine's a little loose," Nancy said. "Let's switch."

Finally everyone had headbands that fit perfectly.

"Where are the feathers?" asked Nancy. "Don't we have to have feathers?"

Mary nodded. "That's the most important part, but it's also the most difficult."

"What's so hard about finding feathers?" said George. "My pillow is full of them."

"It can't be that kind of feather," Mary said. "It has to be a special feather."

"What makes a feather special?" asked Nancy.

"It has to come from a *living* bird," Mary explained.

"You mean we're going to have to pull a feather from a real, live bird?" Bess exclaimed. "How are we going to do that? I don't think we should go around chasing birds, trying to steal their feathers."

"That wouldn't work, either," said Mary, "even if you could catch one. No, it has to be one that the bird left behind, just so it can be used in a ceremony."

"Birds do that?" Nancy said.

"That's what one of our legends says," Mary told them. "A bird will drop a feather some-where, making a connection with the earth, and then we'll pick it up and put it in our head-bands and use it when we're celebrating some-thing important."

"Oh, I love that story," said Nancy.

"So do we," Bess and George chimed in.

"No one else in the pageant will be doing anything like this," Bess said. "All the Pilgrims are making their hats and bonnets out of black construction paper! How boring!"

All of a sudden, the girls heard a loud gasp coming from the kitchen.

"What was that?" Mary asked.

Nancy looked at Bess and George. "It was Hannah! Let's go see what's happening. Come on!"

Hannah Gruen was the Drews' housekeeper. She had been with the family ever since Nancy's mother had died five years before. Nancy was positive that Hannah was the best cook in River Heights. She was also sure that Hannah gave the best hugs.

When the girls got to the kitchen, Hannah was just getting off the phone.

"Are you all right?" Nancy asked.

Hannah turned and looked at them. "I just got off the phone with Mr. Madison," she said sadly. "It looks like Thanksgiving won't be the same this year!"

CHAPTER TWO

Pumpkin Problems

"Oh no!" Bess cried. "It's my favorite holiday!"

"Mine too," said Nancy. "Hannah cooks a great meal, especially the pumpkin pie."

"Forget my pumpkin pie this year," Hannah said. "There won't be any."

The girls looked at one another.

"Why not?" Mary asked.

"Somebody destroyed all of Mr. Madison's jars of pumpkin puree," Hannah explained. She shook her head. "Who would do such a horrible thing?"

Mr. Madison was the father of Katherine Madison, who went to school with the girls. Mr. Madison was also one of the chefs helping to prepare the Thanksgiving feast. It always took place in the school gymnasium, right after the pageant and before the food fair.

"Well, I'm sorry to hear that we won't have pumpkin pies at the feast, Hannah, but what does that have to do with *your* pumpkin pie?" Nancy asked. "Won't there still be cans of pumpkin puree at the market?"

Hannah stared at her. "Nancy Drew, are you telling me that you believed all these years that I was making my pumpkin pies from *canned* pumpkin?"

"Yes," Nancy replied, blushing.

"That's what my mother does," said George. "I thought everybody did."

Hannah shook her head in disbelief. "I only use Mr. Madison's fresh pumpkin puree. That's why my pies have won so many awards," she said. "Mr. Madison uses the puree when he bakes his pies for the feast, and then he sells the remaining jars at the food fair afterward."

"Well, this is terrible, then," Nancy said, "because your pies are the best!"

"We may not be smelling pumpkin pies this year," Bess declared, "but I'm smelling a mystery."

"That's for sure," Nancy said. "Let's get our bikes and head over to the school so we can talk to Mr. Madison."

"Would you like to come with us, Mary?" Bess asked. "The Clue Crew always welcomes other detectives."

Mary looked at the clock on the kitchen wall. "I can't," she said. "I promised Mom I'd clean up my room."

Hannah turned to Nancy. "That's not a bad idea," she said.

"I promise I'll do it as soon as I'm back, Hannah," Nancy said hurriedly. "When a mystery calls, the Clue Crew has to drop everything."

"Well, I'll agree with the *dropping* part," said Hannah. "It looks like that's what you did with all your clothes on the way to your closet."

"Speaking of clothes, we'd better change first,"

George suggested. "People will think the Clue Crew has become the Native American Princess Clue Crew."

"That's for sure," said Bess.

Nancy, Bess, and George said good-bye to Mary, then rushed to Nancy's room to change out of their costumes.

Within minutes, they were biking down the sidewalk toward River Heights Elementary School. The school was only four blocks from Nancy's house, so the girls were allowed to travel there alone, as long as they stayed together.

When they arrived, they left their bikes in the bike rack, locked them up, and headed for the gymnasium. All the doors were open because people were coming and going as they decorated for the upcoming festivities. The large kitchen was off to the left, between the gym and the cafeteria. That was where Nancy knew they'd find Mr. Madison.

"I see Katherine and her father," Bess said. "Katherine!" she shouted. "The Clue Crew is here to help!"

Katherine looked up and waved.

When the girls got closer, Nancy said, "We're sorry about what happened. Hannah is really upset too."

"She's not the only one," said Katherine. "Everyone Dad called felt the same way."

Mr. Madison nodded. "I think half the people in River Heights make their pumpkin pies from my puree."

"Who would do something like this?" Nancy asked.

12

"We think we know," Katherine said.

Nancy, Bess, and George looked at one another.

"You do?" said Nancy.

"Yes. Peter Patino," Katherine answered.

"Oh no!" George said. "He's one of the nicest boys in our class."

"This is terrible," said Bess.

"What makes you think Peter is guilty?" Nancy asked.

"My dad had to fire Peter's uncle James because he kept missing work at the pumpkin farm," Katherine said. "Peter was really upset about it," she added.

"Still, I just can't believe Peter would commit such a crime," Bess said.

"The Clue Crew doesn't convict suspects until we have the evidence," Nancy reminded her. She looked at Mr. Madison. "Do you mind if we look around?" she asked.

"Be my guest," Mr. Madison said.

As Nancy, Bess, and George walked around

the kitchen, Nancy said, "We need to make sure we don't destroy any evidence, so watch where you step."

"What are we looking for?" asked George.

"Footprints in the puree—probably *sneakers*, if Peter did do it," Nancy replied.

For the next several minutes they walked all around the kitchen, searching every inch of the floor in Mr. Madison's assigned area.

Finally, Nancy said, "Well, whoever did this must have stepped where he or she wouldn't leave any prints."

"Hey, look at this!" exclaimed Bess. She pointed to several blobs of pumpkin puree on the floor. "It looks like someone tried to make a finger painting. See these strange scratches?"

"It was probably just some little kid whose

mother or father was down here helping to cook or decorate," Nancy said. "I don't think it's a clue."

"What do we do now?" George wondered.

"We go talk to—," Nancy started to say.

"I found one!" Bess suddenly shouted.

Nancy and George stopped. Bess was standing at a side entrance that led to an alley.

"You found a footprint?" asked Nancy.

"No, I found a brown-and-gray *feather*!" Bess exclaimed. "Now I have one for my headband."

Nancy and George rolled their eyes at each other.

"We're in the middle of an investigation, Bess," George said. "You need to keep your mind on that."

"Come on, let's go find Peter Patino," said Nancy. "We have some questions to ask him."

CHAPTER THREE

Stolen Stuffing

Nancy and the Clue Crew left the school and headed over to Peter Patino's house, which was a couple of blocks away.

"That wind's chilly!" Nancy said. "I knew I should have worn my jacket."

George shivered. "It wasn't this cold when we left your house," she said. "Let's bike faster. We'll get there sooner, and it'll warm us up." Everyone knew that George could outrun—or outbike—anybody at River Heights Elementary School.

"Hey! Wait for me!" shouted Bess. "I'm not the athlete in this group."

When they got to Peter's house, though, Mrs.

Patino told the girls he wasn't there. "Since there was no school today, he said he was going to meet up with Ned Nickerson to talk about forming a bowling league, so he's probably at the bowling alley."

Ned Nickerson was in fourth grade at River Heights Elementary. He and Nancy were good friends.

"We'll bike over there, then," Nancy said.

"We have something important to ask him," Bess added.

"I wish you'd ask him something for me, too," said Mrs. Patino, smiling.

"What's that?" George asked.

"What time will he be home?" Mrs. Patino asked. "He left after breakfast, and he hasn't been back since."

Nancy looked at Bess and George. "That's interesting," she said.

The girls waved good-bye to Mrs. Patino.

"If we see Peter, we'll give him your message," Bess called to her.

When the Clue Crew was too far for Mrs. Patino to hear, Nancy said, "Peter is sounding more like a suspect all the time. If he's been gone since early this morning, he could have destroyed Mr. Madison's jars of pumpkin puree before he met up with Ned."

"We'll soon find out," said George.

When the girls got to the bowling alley, they parked their bikes in a rack, locked them up, and headed inside.

"There's Peter," Bess said, pointing to the last lane.

"Wow!" Nancy exclaimed. "It looks like half the boys in school are here too."

Peter looked up and waved when he saw the three of them walking toward him. "If you want to bowl," he yelled, "you'll have to start your own league."

When the girls reached him, Bess said, "We don't want to bowl, we want to talk to you about pumpkin puree."

"About *what*?" Peter asked.

Nancy looked around. "Could we talk in private?" she asked.

Peter wrinkled his brow. "Oh no, is the Clue Crew on a case now?" he said.

"As a matter of fact, we are, Patino," George told him. "We're investigating the destruction of Mr. Madison's jars of pumpkin puree in the school kitchen."

Peter blinked, then slowly narrowed his eyes. "Are you telling me that you think I did it?" he asked.

"Did you?" asked George.

"Why would I?" Peter said.

"Because Katherine Madison told us that you were upset about your uncle," George explained.

"Yeah, well, I was upset when Mr. Madison fired Uncle James, because it's hard for my uncle to get a job," Peter said, "but you know that I'd never destroy anyone else's property."

"Well, this is a criminal investigation, and that means we have to cover all bases," Bess said. "It's nothing personal, Peter."

Peter looked around. "I have to go," he said. "It's my turn to bowl."

"Wait, Peter! Can you prove you didn't do it?" Nancy asked. "Do you have an alibi?"

"Yeah, I can, and yes, I do," Peter replied. He turned and called, "Nickerson!"

Ned quickly hurried over to them. "Hi, Nancy! Hi, Bess, George. What are you guys doing here?"

"We're on a case," said Bess.

"And I'm a suspect," Peter said, "but I was just explaining to Nancy that you and I have been busy all day, recruiting guys for the bowling team."

"You think Peter committed a crime?" Ned said. "Come on, Nancy! Get real!"

"Well, we need Peter's alibi," Nancy replied.

"Sure thing. We started out really early this morning, looking for guys, and now we have a team that's going to burn the competition," Ned said.

"Good for you, Ned," said Nancy. She turned

to Bess and George. "I guess we'd better be going."

"Good luck with the investigation," Peter called to them as the girls headed out the door.

"Now what?" Bess asked.

Nancy looked at her watch. "Oh no! I forgot to ask Peter what time he'll be home, and I need to get home too," she said. "It's almost time for dinner, and I promised Hannah I'd clean my room!"

Nancy's father, Carson Drew, was a successful lawyer, so Nancy often discussed some of the

Clue Crew's cases with him. Over dinner, she told Mr. Drew and Hannah about their investigation.

"We thought Peter Patino was a suspect, but it turns out he has an alibi," Nancy said. She sighed. "We'd go back to the crime scene to look for other clues, but by now it's probably been compromised."

"What?" said Hannah.

Nancy grinned. "I heard it on television. That means people have probably walked all over the clues and destroyed them."

"Well, you've been in situations like this before, Nancy. You know that sooner or later evidence will turn up that'll help you solve the crime," Mr. Drew said. "Just keep on sleuthing!"

"The Clue Crew never gives up, Daddy!" Nancy assured him.

The next afternoon, Saturday, Nancy and the Clue Crew met Mary White Cloud at the gymnasium. Mrs. White Cloud was going to help them with their parts in the pageant when she finished making her Indian fry bread. While they were waiting, Nancy and the Clue Crew filled Mary in on what they'd found out about Mr. Madison's pumpkin puree.

"We didn't find any clues," Bess said, "but"—she pulled the feather out from behind her and showed it to Mary—"I did find this. It was left by some bird in the alley outside the school kitchen."

"That's wonderful! You're the first person to pick up a feather, Bess," Mary said. "That's special in our culture."

Bess beamed.

"I'm glad your mother wants to help us with our lines," said Nancy.

"Well, my mom has been in a lot of Native American pageants all across the country," Mary told them proudly.

"She knows how we should act."

Just then, they heard a commotion coming from the kitchen.

Nancy looked at everyone. "Come on!" she shouted. "Let's find out what's going on!"

When they got there, Mrs. White Cloud was talking to Mrs. Stanley, who owned a bakery in town.

"What happened?" asked Nancy.

"I just discovered that somebody got into the storeroom where I had put my special bags of turkey stuffing mix," Mrs. Stanley said. "They ruined every one of them!"

"Oh no, not again!" Nancy groaned. "Someone really is trying to destroy the River Heights Thanksgiving Celebration!"

CHAPTER FOUR

Disastrous Decision

"This is awful," Bess said.

"It most certainly is," Mrs. White Cloud agreed. "Everyone in River Heights has told me nothing tastes as good as Mrs. Stanley's special turkey stuffing mix, and I was really looking forward to eating it."

"Mom uses your special stuffing in our turkey every Thanksgiving," Bess told Mrs. Stanley. "She's going to be so upset."

George sniffed the air. "What's that smell?" she asked.

"Burned cake," Mrs. Stanley said. "Don't ask. It's a long story."

Nancy turned to Mary. "Could we practice

later?" she asked. "This mystery is getting more mysterious, and the Clue Crew needs to check it out."

Mary turned to her mother. "Is that all right?" she asked.

"It most certainly is," said Mrs. White Cloud. "I can teach the girls how to be Native American princesses any time, but the mystery of what happened to the stuffing mix can't wait." To Mary, she added, "The fry bread is done. We need to go on home now, but we'll come back later."

Mary and Mrs. White Cloud said their good-byes and left.

Just then, a huge black dog raced through the kitchen. He had white powder all over his nose. He made a couple of circles and then headed into the gym.

"Wasn't that Quincy Taylor's dog?" George said.

"I think so," said Nancy. "I wonder what he's doing down here."

"Quincy told me his dog has been jumping over their fence lately," Bess said. "He's afraid someone will dognap him if he doesn't stop that."

Nancy turned back to Mrs. Stanley. "Maybe we can solve the mystery of who destroyed your stuffing mix," she said. "We haven't solved Mr. Madison's crime yet, but we're still working on it."

"The two could be related," Bess pointed out.

Mrs. Stanley blinked in surprise. "What do you mean?" she asked.

"Mr. Madison's pumpkin puree was destroyed in this same kitchen yesterday," George reasoned. "We're investigating that case too."

"I hadn't heard about that. I was working in my bakery, trying to get caught up with holiday orders," Mrs. Stanley said. "That's just terrible! I use his pumpkin puree for my pumpkin pies."

"How did you discover that something had happened to your stuffing mix?" asked Nancy.

"Well, I came here to the school to do my part for the feast, but I also needed to bake a couple of holiday cakes for a customer," Mrs. Stanley explained, "so I put one in the oven, and then I started making the second one, but I was listening to my favorite station on the radio at the same time, not paying as much attention to what I was doing as I should, and I burned the first cake."

Bess sniffed the air again and nodded to George.

"So I opened the door to the alley, to let in some fresh air, and then I went back to work on the cakes," Mrs. Stanley continued. "When I finally finished with those, it was time to start adding the wet ingredients, such as turkey broth, to the dry stuffing mix for the feast, and that's when I discovered that someone had knocked over all the bags and scattered the stuffing mix all over the floor."

"Can you make some more?" Nancy asked.

Mrs. Stanley shook her head. "Unfortunately, no. I use specially aged bread crumbs and just the right seasoning. It takes a while. There's not enough time left between now and the feast."

"I think I know who's responsible for these crimes!" George shouted. "Quincy's dog!"

"Yeah!" Bess agreed. "He sure did look guilty when he raced through just now."

"Maybe he came through the door to the alley and got into the stuffing mix when you weren't paying attention, Mrs. Stanley," Nancy said. She turned to Bess and George. "I wonder if he's responsible for destroying Mr. Madison's pumpkin puree, too."

"We should find out if he has an alibi for that time," George said.

"We'll do that after we examine the crime scene," Nancy decided.

The Clue Crew started looking for clues.

After a few minutes George said, "I'm going to look out in the alley."

Nancy and Bess continued to search the storeroom and kitchen.

When George came back inside, she said, "Well, I know why Quincy's dog's nose was all white. There's a flour spill in the alley from where he was digging around in the trash can."

Nancy looked at the spilled bags of stuffing mix on the floor. "If Quincy's dog were the culprit, wouldn't there be signs of flour on some of

the bags in either the storeroom or the kitchen where he nosed them open?" she asked.

"You'd think," George said.

"Well, there aren't," Nancy told her friends.

"What if he came in here first?" asked Bess.

"I think someone would have noticed him earlier if he had come into the kitchen first," Nancy concluded. "I don't think Quincy's dog is our criminal."

"Another dead end." Bess sighed.

"Not for me," said George. She held up a feather. "I found one in the alley too, just like Bess did. Now I have a feather for the pageant!"

Later that evening, when Nancy and the Clue Crew went back to the gymnasium to practice their roles, the first thing George did was tell Mary about finding her brown-and-gray feather.

Mary let out a sigh. "You may not get to use it after all," she said.

"What do you mean?" Nancy asked.

"Well, Deirdre Shannon's parents are in charge of this year's celebration," Mary explained. "After they heard about the food being destroyed, they told Mrs. Ramirez that the entire event—the pageant, the feast, and the food fair—might have to be canceled. They're worried it's turning into a disaster."

Chapter Five

Cold Case

On Sunday afternoon, before Nancy left for the school to practice for the pageant, she told her father everything that had happened the day before.

"Do you think the two crimes could be a coincidence, Daddy?" Nancy asked.

"Well, there are such things as coincidences, Nancy, and the two might not be related after all," said Mr. Drew. "But don't give up on finding the culprits. Just follow the evidence and remember that things aren't always as they appear."

"Don't worry, Daddy," Nancy said. "The Clue Crew is still on the case! See you later." She grabbed her jacket and headed out the door.

When Nancy got to the school, some of the other kids who had parts in the pageant were gathered in little groups on the playground. They were whispering to one another about the possible cancellation.

"Don't worry," Nancy reassured the kids as she passed each group. "The Clue Crew is trying to solve the mystery."

Nancy finally found George and Bess by the swings. They were talking with Katherine Madison, Suzie Park, and Natalie Coleman.

"George and I found the perfect feathers, too," Bess was saying when Nancy joined them. "But if the celebration is canceled, we won't be able to use them in the pageant."

"Oh, that would be too bad," Natalie said.

"I love this time of the year," said Suzie, "mainly because of the celebration."

"Me too," Katherine said. "My dad and I were already upset about his pumpkin puree, and now if everything is canceled, we'll feel even worse."

"Try not to worry too much, girls," Nancy told them. "The Clue Crew hasn't given up!"

As Nancy, Bess, and George entered the school gym, Nancy said, "There's Mrs. Ramirez over by the stage. I need to talk to her. I'm going to run on ahead."

Mrs. Ramirez looked up when Nancy reached her. "Oh, hi, Nancy," she said sadly. "I suppose you've heard the news that the celebration may be canceled."

"It hasn't happened yet, Mrs. Ramirez," Nancy said, "and the Clue Crew is going to do everything possible to make sure that it doesn't."

"Thank you, Nancy!" said Mrs. Ramirez.

Just then, Deirdre Shannon walked up. "Oh, Nancy, isn't it just awful?" she said.

"Isn't *what* awful, Deirdre?" Nancy said.

"You haven't heard?" Deirdre exclaimed. "There may not be a River Heights Thanksgiving Celebration this year after all."

"Oh, *that*." Nancy smiled. "Well, the Clue Crew is on the case, Deirdre."

"That would be awesome if you solved it, because everyone is working so hard," she said. "I'm in charge of costumes for all the Pilgrim girls, and I'm trying my best to make them look stylish in those boring black dresses."

"Well, Deirdre, if anyone knows about fashion, it's you," said Nancy. "But I don't know if there's a lot you can do about what the Pilgrim women wore back then."

"You're probably right," Deirdre said. "I wish the Thanksgiving pageant was set in Paris or New York during Fashion Week."

"Don't count on that happening!" Nancy joked.

"Well, I have to go get my mom's fresh turkeys," Deirdre said. "Normally, she has to wait until the food fair, but Mr. Davidson, our butcher, said she could get hers today because she and Dad are so busy coordinating the celebration."

"Do you need any help?" Nancy asked.

"Sure," Deirdre said. "Those turkeys are heavy."

Nancy turned to Mrs. Ramirez. "Do we have time before the pageant practice starts?" she asked.

"Well, if the Clue Crew is going to save the celebration, then we'll have practice," Mrs. Ramirez said, "so we can certainly wait until you've finished helping Deirdre with the turkeys."

Nancy and Deirdre headed toward the kitchen. When they got to Mr. Davidson's area, he wasn't anywhere to be found.

"I can't wait for him," Deirdre said. "I have so many things to do."

"Where does he keep the turkeys?" asked Nancy.

"They're fresh turkeys, not frozen," Deirdre explained, "so he just keeps them in his refrigerator."

"Well, there's a big refrigerator over there," Nancy said. "The door's wide open."

They walked over and looked inside.

"Here are two big turkeys with my mom's name on them," Deirdre said. "I guess it's all right to take them."

Deirdre picked up one of the turkeys. "Yuck! It's all squishy, like it's still alive!"

"Let me see," Nancy said. Deirdre handed her the turkey. "You're right. It's not even cold."

Just then, a voice said, "What are you two doing?"

Nancy and Deirdre turned. Mr. Davidson was staring at them.

"I think someone left the door to your refrigerator open, Mr. Davidson," said Nancy.

Mr. Davidson rushed over. He took the turkey from Nancy. "Oh no!" he cried. He examined the other turkeys in the refrigerator. "They're all spoiled! Now all my butcher shop customers will have to eat *frozen* turkeys for Thanksgiving!"

"Oh, that's terrible!" Deirdre said. "I guess my parents really will have to cancel the—"

"Wait, Deirdre! Please don't say anything to them yet!" Nancy interrupted. "Just give the Clue Crew a little more time. We'll get back on the case right now!"

ChaPTER Six

Clueless Clues

Just then, George and Bess came into the kitchen.

"We wondered what had happened to you," Bess said. "Mrs. Ramirez is ready for us to practice."

"Our plans have changed," Nancy told her friends. She quickly explained about the spoiled turkeys. "Somebody really is out to destroy Thanksgiving. This is no coincidence!"

"Why couldn't they attack some other holiday?" asked Bess. "Why did they have to choose my favorite one?"

"Thanksgiving is a holiday for people to give *thanks* for all they have," Nancy said. "That makes it doubly awful that someone is trying to wreck the celebration!"

"I agree," George said.

"Would you mind if we took a look around, Mr. Davidson?" Nancy asked. "The Clue Crew is investigating the other kitchen crimes."

"I wouldn't mind it at all, Nancy," Mr. Davidson replied. He was a big fan of the Clue Crew. "Nothing like this has ever happened before."

"Well, I need to go. . . . The pageant will go on!" said Deirdre.

"Tell your mother I'm sorry about the turkeys," Mr. Davidson said. "I'll make sure it doesn't happen next year."

When Deirdre was gone, Nancy said, "Do you know any reason why someone would do this, Mr. Davidson?"

Mr. Davidson shook his head. "No. In fact, I try to be nice to everybody. When Mr. Shannon said he was expecting a late delivery of cranberries and potatoes from a wholesale packer in Chicago, I told him I'd be glad to stay to make sure everything was put away. I left the back door open so the driver could bring the boxes inside, because I was busy preparing the fresh turkeys."

Bess looked at Nancy. "I wonder if we can connect the driver to the other crimes," she said.

"I know him. He's not a crook," said Mr. Davidson. "The way I see it, while he was busy bringing the boxes, someone slipped inside and hid until after I was gone and then committed the crime."

"Maybe the deliveryman left the refrigerator door open by mistake, and you didn't notice it," George suggested. "Maybe he was in a hurry and just didn't get it closed."

"No. He put the cranberries and potatoes in one of the storerooms," Mr. Davidson said. "He didn't need to open the refrigerator door. Anyway, I'm sure it was closed when I left early this morning."

Nancy walked over to the refrigerator and examined the handle. It didn't look very sturdy, and she was sure it wouldn't take much effort to open the door. The handle was also right next to the edge of a long table, which had several small white feathers and a *brown-and-gray* one beneath it.

"Is this where you plucked your turkeys, Mr. Davidson?" Nancy asked.

"It's one of the places," Mr. Davidson answered.

"What color were the feathers of your turkeys?" she asked.

"They were all white," Mr. Davidson said. "Why?"

"I was just curious, that's all," Nancy said.

She couldn't believe it. The brown-and-gray feather was just like the ones Bess and George had found at the other crime scenes. She quickly put it into her pocket.

"Well, I guess we'd better be going," she said. "I think there's something we need to investigate." She turned to Bess and George. "Come on, let's go."

Once outside, Nancy took the feather out of her pocket and showed it to them.

"Wow!" Bess said. "Now all three of us have feathers!"

"That's not the point, Bess," Nancy said.

"It isn't?" said George.

"No," Nancy said. "Do you realize that we've found the same kind of feather at all three crime scenes?"

"Oh yeah!" Bess remembered.

"I think the thief is using feathers as his calling card," Nancy said. "He—or she—wants us to find them so we'll know it's the same person committing the crimes."

"Why?" George asked.

"Some criminals like to be known by things like that," Nancy explained. "When they read about 'the Feather Bandit' in the newspaper, they feel special."

"That's true!" Bess said. "You see it on television all the time!"

"Right!" George put in. She looked at Nancy. "What are we going to do about it?"

"We're going to tell Mrs. Ramirez that we need to do some sleuthing instead of practicing our parts, and then we're going to my house to do a little research on the Internet," Nancy said. "I want to find out if there have been crimes in other towns where feathers have been left."

ChAPTER SEVEN

Funny Feathers

The Internet didn't turn up anything on "feather bandits," so Nancy and the Clue Crew took their feathers to Mary White Cloud's house.

"This is the third time we've found a feather at the scene of a crime," Nancy told her. "We think it's the thief's calling card."

"Oh, I've heard about that on television," Mary said. She sighed. "I'm sorry, but if these feathers did come from a thief and we have the pageant, I don't think you can use them."

"Why not?" George asked.

"Well, if they were dropped by a thief instead of a bird," Mary explained, "then that means they're negative, not positive, and you always need to use positive feathers in a pageant when you're dealing with Native American culture."

"That makes sense," Nancy said. Bess and George nodded.

"We'll just have to start all over," said Bess. She looked at her feather. "It was so pretty, too."

"Do you know what kind of feathers these are, Mary?" Nancy asked.

Mary shook her head. "No, I don't. We don't always know what kind of a bird drops its feathers, but in our culture, it doesn't really matter, as long as the bird does it willingly." She looked at Nancy. "Is it important to your investigation?" she asked.

"I think it could be," Nancy said. She looked at Bess and George. "It might give us a clue as to who the thief is, if we knew where the feathers came from."

"What if the thief is just picking them up off the ground like we were doing?" asked Bess. "It might mean nothing."

"Or it might mean *something*," George said. "I

agree with Nancy. We should check this out."

"Well, you could ask Mrs. Fulton," Mary suggested. "She teaches science, so she might know about birds."

"That's a great idea," Nancy said. She looked at her watch. "We still have time. It won't be dark for another hour."

They used Mary's telephone to ask Mrs. Fulton if they could come over because they had something very important to talk to her about. She told them they could.

"See you later, Mary!" the girls shouted.

Nancy and the Clue Crew headed to Mrs. Fulton's house, which was down the street from Mary's.

When they arrived, Nancy rang the buzzer.

Mrs. Fulton opened the door. "Goodness, that was quick!" she exclaimed. "Come on in, girls."

The girls headed through the door.

"Well, to what do I owe the honor of your presence, Nancy Drew and the Clue Crew?" Mrs. Fulton said. "I don't think either my husband or I have committed a crime, although some of my students probably don't agree with me after that last test I gave them."

"We found some feathers," Nancy said. "We were hoping you could identify them for us."

"Well, I may be able to, if they're not too exotic," Mrs. Fulton said. "I studied ornithology in college, actually."

"Orni-*what*?" Bess asked.

"That's the study of birds, Bess," George said.

Nancy pulled the three brown-and-gray feathers out of her pocket and handed them to Mrs. Fulton. "Do you recognize them?" she asked.

Mrs. Fulton grinned. "Is this a Thanksgiving prank?" she said.

Nancy looked at Bess and George. "No, we're very serious," she said. "I'd rather not tell you where we found them, since it's part of an ongoing investigation, but we thought that you, as the expert, could help us with the case."

"Of course," Mrs. Fulton said. "They're wild turkey feathers."

"*Wild turkey* feathers?" the girls exclaimed.

"You're kidding," Nancy said.

Mrs. Fulton looked at the feathers again. "Nope, that's what they are," she confirmed.

"Well," Nancy said. She bit her lip in thought. "This is starting to make sense now. You've really helped—"

Just then, a man burst through the front door. "LOUISE! My green beans are ruined!"

Nancy and her friends looked at Mrs. Fulton.

"It's my husband," she said.

Nancy looked at Mr. Fulton. "Were your green beans at the elementary school, by any chance?" she asked.

Mr. Fulton nodded.

"Oh no," Bess said.

"Not again!" George added.

"What are you talking about?" Mrs. Fulton asked.

"We've seen this happen before," Nancy told her. She turned to Mr. Fulton. "Were your green beans supposed to be for the Thanksgiving feast?" she asked.

Mr. Fulton's mouth dropped open. "Yes, but how did you know?" he said.

"It's a long story," Nancy told him. "Can you tell us what happened?"

"My poor green beans! I work so hard in the summer, tending to them carefully, then canning them when they're ready, and then I put them in my garage until I take them to the school for the River Heights Thanksgiving Celebration," Mr. Fulton said. "People love my green beans!"

"Oh yes!" Bess said. "They're delicious, and I don't even like green beans."

"Let me guess. Somebody got into one of the storerooms and knocked all the jars off the shelves," said Nancy, "and now there won't be any, right?"

Mr. Fulton blinked. "Right," he said.

"Did you find any feathers at the scene of the crime?" Nancy asked.

"Yes, as a matter of fact, I did," Mr. Fulton said. "Wow! You girls really are great detectives!" He pulled some brown-and-gray feathers out of his pocket and handed them to Mrs. Fulton. "Do you recognize these?"

"Yes, they're wild turkey feathers," Mrs. Fulton said. She turned to Nancy and the Clue Crew. "Does this have anything to do with your investigation?" she asked.

"Yes, it does," Nancy told her. "We're looking for a person who wants to destroy the River Heights Thanksgiving Celebration and who leaves a wild turkey feather at the scene of each crime!"

ChaPTER EiGhT

Turkey Talk

The next morning, Monday, when Nancy's alarm went off, she sat up and stretched. The first thing she thought was, *We need to find out who in River Heights would have access to a lot of wild turkey feathers, and we'll solve the case.*

With that in mind, Nancy hopped out of bed, put on her robe and slippers, and, as she did every morning, opened her drapes to let in the sun.

Suddenly she gasped. Two wild turkeys were down on the front lawn, pecking at the dead grass, their bright red wattles flapping in the wind.

"Oh, wow!" Nancy exclaimed. "What are you two . . ."

Nancy didn't finish her sentence. All of a sudden, she was sure she was looking at the solution to the mystery the Clue Crew was investigating! But she also knew she had no real evidence—unless you could count the three wild turkey feathers—and how could she prove that they came from these two turkeys?

"I have to take you both into custody," Nancy whispered. "You may not like it, but if you two are out to destroy the River Heights Thanksgiving

Celebration, then the Clue Crew is going to stop you!"

Of course, what would happen once she had them in custody? Nancy wondered. How in the world would she ever figure out if they were missing any of their feathers? *Do feathers grow back?* Nancy thought. *Wow, these crimes get more and more complicated around here!* Still, it had to be done, Nancy knew. She slowly closed the drapes so she wouldn't spook the turkeys if they happened to glance at her upstairs window.

Next, Nancy hurriedly called both Bess and George and told them the same thing: "You're absolutely not going to believe this. You have to come to my house right away! And use the back door!"

Then Nancy returned to the window and peeked out again. For a minute she panicked because the two wild turkeys weren't where they had been, but she craned her neck and saw that they were over by a tree on the far side of the yard.

Suddenly the turkeys flapped their wings, as though they were trying to fly but couldn't. Then they headed for the street.

"Oh my gosh!" Nancy cried. "They're escaping!"

Nancy dressed quickly, then raced downstairs.

As she started for the front door, Hannah called, "Where are you going without your breakfast, Nancy Drew?"

"I'm on a case, Hannah! I don't have time for food!" Nancy said as she unlocked the door. At that moment, someone rang the back doorbell, and Nancy was sure it was Bess and George. "Please tell them to come this way, Hannah! I'm chasing two turkeys down the street!"

"You're *what*?" Hannah cried.

But Nancy was already running down the front porch steps. She could still see the turkeys. They were trotting down the middle of the street. A car coming toward them swerved to keep from hitting them.

"Nancy!" Bess called out from the front yard. "What's going on?"

"Hurry up!" Nancy shouted back. "I'll explain on the way!"

Just as Bess and George reached Nancy, the turkeys decided to change direction.

"They're headed for Suzie's front yard!" Nancy said.

"So what?" said Bess.

"So I think they're the ones who're trying to destroy Thanksgiving in River Heights!" Nancy replied.

"*Turkeys?*" said George.

"Yeah, *wild* turkeys," Nancy said.

Nancy and the Clue Crew reached Suzie's house just in time to see the turkeys fly over the side fence.

"I didn't know turkeys could fly," Bess said.

"They can't fly very far," George said.

"Yeah, just enough to create problems for us," said Nancy. "Come on!"

They ran toward the gate that led to Suzie's backyard.

"Maybe Suzie can help us," Bess said.

Nancy looked at her watch. "She's probably already at school. She likes to get there early to use the library."

George glanced down at her watch too. "That's where we should be, Nancy, *at school*!" she said. "Mrs. Ramirez said we were going to have a math quiz first thing."

Nancy had forgotten that. She needed a good grade on this one, too, because she had missed several problems on the previous quiz.

Now the girls were inside Suzie's backyard, and the turkeys were running around, looking for a way to escape.

"I think we have them," George said. "Here, turkey, turkey! Here, turkey, turkey!"

Suddenly the turkeys raced for the back fence, flapped their wings a couple of times, and were gone.

"Oh, great," Nancy said. "Well, let's see if we can find them on the next block!"

George pointed to her watch. "The time, Nancy, the time!" she said.

"We have to do this, guys!" Nancy told her friends. "We can't let them destroy Thanksgiving!"

Bess turned to George. "Nancy's right," she said. "We owe it to the citizens of River Heights, and that includes Mrs. Ramirez and her family!"

The Clue Crew raced out of Suzie's backyard, up to the corner, and over to the next street, where they saw the turkeys trotting down the center of the road.

"They're not going very fast," said Nancy. "They probably think they outsmarted us."

"They could also just be tired," George pointed out.

Just then, one of the turkeys turned its head and looked right at the girls. It made a loud gobbling sound to the other turkey, and the other turkey gobbled back. Then the two of them took off.

"What do you think they said?" Bess asked.

"The first one said, 'You're not going to believe

this, but they're behind us again!'" Nancy said,
"and the second one said, 'You've got to be kidding me!'"

"I had no idea you understood turkey talk!"
Bess giggled.

"Oh yeah," Nancy replied. "Come on."

For the next twenty minutes, the Clue Crew
chased the turkeys all around the neighbor-
hood, but then the birds seemed to vanish into
thin air.

"Look at us," Bess said. "We're all sweaty and
messy!"

Nancy glanced down at her clothes. "You're right. We need to go home and change."

"No, we don't," George said. "At least this way, Mrs. Ramirez might believe the story we're going to tell her."

As it turned out, Mrs. Ramirez did believe their story, but they still had to stay after school to take the test, and because they had missed part of school, their parents were also called.

"This is kind of embarrassing, Nancy," said Bess.

"Well, what's really embarrassing, Bess, is that we failed to catch the turkeys," Nancy said. She sighed. "If there's no Thanksgiving Celebration this year, then it'll be our fault."

CHAPTER NINE

Sad Setting

When Nancy got home, Hannah said, "The school called. Your father will be upset that you got there so late." She shook her head. "I certainly hope you didn't look like that all day!"

Nancy told Hannah about chasing the wild turkeys all over their part of town. "I'm sure they're the ones responsible for what's been going on, but the only evidence we have so far are three feathers."

"Some evidence," said Hannah. She took a deep breath, let it out, then added, "Well, why don't you clean up before dinner?"

"Okay," Nancy said. She looked around. "Where's Dad?"

"He's working late at the office," Hannah told her.

"Oh, darn!" Nancy said. "I wanted to talk to him about the case."

"Well, it'll have to wait until morning," Hannah said, "because I have strict orders that you're not to stay up until he gets home."

Nancy was so tired, she didn't argue this time. Chasing two wild turkeys around River Heights was not something she did every day.

When Nancy awakened on Tuesday morning, she opened her drapes in hopes that the two turkeys had returned. But she saw only dead leaves being scattered by the wind.

Mr. Drew was already at the breakfast table, drinking his coffee and reading the newspaper, when Nancy went downstairs.

Nancy gave him a big hug, then sat down next to him and drank half the glass of orange juice Hannah had already put by her plate.

"I'm sorry about being late to school yesterday," Nancy apologized.

"It's not like you, Nancy, so I'm guessing you must have had a good reason. Hannah said you had something important to tell me about your current investigation," Mr. Drew said.

Nancy told him about the wild turkey chase. "But we finally lost them," she finished, "and we don't know where they went."

Mr. Drew thought for a minute. "So you think these two turkeys are responsible for all the destruction?" he said.

"Well, Daddy, it's really just a hunch, since the only evidence we have are three wild turkey feathers," Nancy told him. "But the fact that the turkeys were in town makes them suspicious."

"You're right about that, Nancy," Mr. Drew said. "I have an idea. I think I know where we might find these two birds—provided, of course, that they are responsible."

"Really?" Nancy said. "Can you take us there after school?"

Mr. Drew drained his coffee cup and replied, "Of course!"

That afternoon Bess and George went home with Nancy, where Hannah gave them an after-school snack. Then Mr. Drew drove them to the new city park, two blocks from River Heights Elementary School.

Nancy looked around, puzzled. "Why are we here, Daddy?"

"This is the only part left of what used to be a large area of wilderness. It used to stretch way out into the countryside," Mr. Drew explained.

"Really?" Nancy said.

Mr. Drew nodded. "This whole area was once all trees and bushes," he told the girls. He stopped the car. "Let's get out and look around. We'll need to be quiet, just in case our friends are around here, and I think they are."

"Friends?" asked Nancy.

"I don't consider anyone trying to destroy Thanksgiving a *friend*," Bess added.

"Me either," George put in.

"Don't be so quick to judge," said Mr. Drew. "There are always two sides to every story."

For the next several minutes, the four of them made their way through the thick underbrush, trying to be as quiet as possible.

Suddenly Mr. Drew held a finger up to his lips, warning them not to make a sound. He slowly pulled apart a couple of branches and peered between them. "Nancy, look at this," he whispered.

"Oh my gosh!" Nancy whispered back. "I don't believe it."

Bess and George took turns looking. Then the four of them moved back, away from the thicket, so they could talk about what they had seen.

"They're the crooks, all right, Nancy," George said. "We've solved another case."

"Right," Nancy said. "We caught them red-handed with the evidence."

In the thicket, Nancy had seen the two adult wild turkeys, along with three offspring. They were surrounded by a bag of stuffing mix, some dried pumpkin puree, and piles of green beans.

"But that still doesn't explain who opened the refrigerator door and ruined all of Mr. Davidson's fresh turkeys," Bess said.

"Oh, I think it does, Bess," Nancy said. "If those turkeys are strong enough to carry some of that food here to the thicket, then I'm sure they'd be strong enough to fly up on that table where I found the feather and open the refrigerator handle with a foot or a beak."

"Wow!" George said. "I'm impressed with how smart they are!"

"Animals will do whatever it takes to survive," Nancy said. "Of course, they were probably shocked when they found other turkeys in the refrigerator!"

"Well, yeah!" Bess said.

Nancy turned to her father. "How did you know the turkeys would be here, Dad?" she asked.

"Well, like I told you, Nancy, this whole area used to be wilderness," Mr. Drew explained. "It was home to a lot of wildlife, including wild turkeys. Come over here," he said. "I want to show you something else."

They walked several yards to the edge of the park. They saw a group of new homes. "These housing additions were built where a lot of wild animals used to live," Mr. Drew said. "Now there's not enough land left to support them."

Nancy turned to Bess and George. "Well, the Clue Crew solved the mystery of who was trying to destroy Thanksgiving in River Heights," she said, "but now we have another problem. . . ."

CHAPTER TEN

Smart Solution

At school on Wednesday morning, the day of the festival, Mrs. Ramirez said, "Nancy Drew has an announcement to make."

Nancy came to the front of the room. "The people who were trying to destroy the River Heights Thanksgiving Celebration aren't people," she began. "They're *wild turkeys*."

The class gasped.

"Oh, I saw them on television!" Deirdre said. "They were drinking dirty water from that broken pipe here at our school."

"Right!" said Nancy.

She then told the class about the disappearing wilderness. She talked about how the Clue Crew had seen the wild turkeys in the last remaining thicket trying to feed their young.

"That's terrible," Katherine Madison said. "We can't let this happen to them."

"We need to do something about it," said Deirdre.

The rest of the class agreed.

"Well, here's my plan," Nancy said. "My dad says there is some land on the other side of the river. We're going to ask the City of River Heights to buy that land so the local wildlife, including turkeys, will have a place to live."

The class cheered.

"Why hasn't the wildlife already gone there?" Peter Patino asked.

"The river's probably too wide for some of them to swim across," George guessed. "But we honestly didn't ask them that question."

The class laughed.

"The wild turkeys will have a place to live and raise their families," Bess said. "And they won't have to come over to our school to steal food!"

"What will they do until we get the wildlife refuge ready?" Katherine asked.

"That brings me to the second part of my plan," Nancy continued. "We're going to feed them in the park every week until the wildlife refuge is ready. Who's with me?"

All the hands in the class went up.

While Nancy was making a list of volunteers, a couple of the other teachers came into the room. They huddled with Mrs. Ramirez, then left.

Mrs. Ramirez quieted down the class. "The other classes want to be involved too, Nancy, so we should have plenty of volunteers to make sure the turkeys are fed until they can be moved," she said.

Nancy grinned.

"Now, then, class, we're going to the gym to practice for the pageant," Mrs. Ramirez said. "I hope you haven't forgotten that the Thanksgiving Celebration is tonight."

"We haven't!" the class shouted.

That night Nancy, Bess, George, and Mary White Cloud were huddled in the wings behind the curtain.

George pulled the curtain back to peek out. "Oh, wow!" she said. "This place is packed."

"Let me look at you," said Mary. She adjusted their headbands. "Perfect. You really do look like Native American princesses."

"Do you have our turkey feathers?" Bess asked.

Mary nodded. "Your three and one Mr. Fulton gave me!" she said.

"Super!" Nancy said.

"I am now going to perform the feather ritual," Mary said. "I will put one feather at the back of each headband."

"Places, princesses," Mrs. Ramirez whispered. "You're on in two minutes."

Nancy Drew and the Clue Crew lined up behind Mary.

"I wonder if we would have found any feathers if those wild turkeys hadn't tried to destroy Thanksgiving," Bess whispered.

"I don't really believe now that they were trying to destroy Thanksgiving, Bess," Nancy whispered back. "I think they were just trying to get our attention."

"Well, they certainly did that," George said with a smile.

Then, on cue, the four Native American princesses walked out onto the stage, where they were welcomed by the Pilgrims.

Pumpkin Pie Pomander

A pomander is a mixture of great-smelling things packaged in a paper ball. A pumpkin pie pomander will make you think it's Thanksgiving all year when you hang it inside your closet or put it in a drawer.

You will need:

One orange

Two boxes of dried cloves

One tin or jar of pumpkin pie spice

Two sheets of tissue paper

Ten to twelve inches of orange or brown grosgrain (narrow) ribbon

One plastic food-storage bag

Two sheets of stickers with gold or silver stars and half moons, or two sheets with stickers that would appeal to one of your friends, if you plan to give the pomander as a gift!

❀ Before you start, you need to put on an apron, and then cover the kitchen table with newspaper. It's probably a good idea to secure the newspaper with tape. Then, when it's time to clean up, you can simply wad up the newspaper and throw it into the trash.

❀ First, stick the cloves into the orange, pushing them down as far as they'll go, until the entire surface is covered.

❈ Next, put the pumpkin pie spice in the food-storage bag. Add the clove-studded orange and shake gently until the orange is covered with the spice.

❈ Then wrap the orange in the tissue paper, tie it up with the orange or brown ribbon, and put it in a warm, dry place for about a month. When the orange is dried out, the pomander is ready to make your room smell like it's full of pumpkin pies!

❈ Now decorate the tissue paper with the stickers, and you're all set!

SECRET FILES

THE HARDY BOYS®

Follow the trail with Frank and Joe Hardy
in this new chapter book mystery series!

SECRET FILES #1

THE HARDY BOYS

Trouble at the Arcade

BY FRANKLIN W. DIXON   ILLUSTRATED BY SCOTT BURROUGHS

SECRET FILES #2

THE HARDY BOYS

The Missing Mitt

BY FRANKLIN W. DIXON   ILLUSTRATED BY SCOTT BURROUGHS

SECRET FILES #3

THE HARDY BOYS

Mystery Map

BY FRANKLIN W. DIXON   ILLUSTRATED BY SCOTT BURROUGHS

SECRET FILES #4

THE HARDY BOYS

Hopping Mad

BY FRANKLIN W. DIXON   ILLUSTRATED BY SCOTT BURROUGHS

SECRET FILES #5

THE HARDY BOYS

A Monster of a Mystery

BY FRANKLIN W. DIXON   ILLUSTRATED BY SCOTT BURROUGHS

BY FRANKLIN W. DIXON

FROM ALADDIN • PUBLISHED BY
SIMON & SCHUSTER

Mermaid Tales

Can't get enough of the
Trident Academy merkids?
Visit MermaidTalesBooks.com
for activities, excerpts, and more!

NANCY DREW
AND THE CLUE CREW®

Can you solve these other mysteries
from Nancy Drew and the Clue Crew?

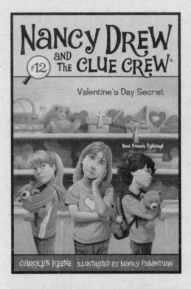

NANCY DREW
#12 AND THE CLUE CREW

Valentine's Day Secret

Best friends fighting!

CAROLYN KEENE ILLUSTRATED BY MACKY PAMINTUAN

NANCY DREW
#13 AND THE CLUE CREW

Chick-napped!

Crack this case!

CAROLYN KEENE ILLUSTRATED BY MACKY PAMINTUAN

NANCY DREW
#14 AND THE CLUE CREW

The Zoo Crew

Oversight at the zoo!

CAROLYN KEENE ILLUSTRATED BY MACKY PAMINTUAN

NANCY DREW
#15 AND THE CLUE CREW

Mall Madness

A shopping mystery!

CAROLYN KEENE ILLUSTRATED BY MACKY PAMINTUAN

For more Sparkle Spa fun including
polls, nail designs, and more
visit SparkleSpaBooks.com!

ALADDIN